One morning, a van stopped outside the house. A man got out, unloaded a big box, and wheeled it up to the house.

The big box was addressed to Jess and Zack's dad. It was as tall as Jess. She and Zack looked at it as it stood in the hall.

"What is inside it?" said Zack.

"I suppose we will have to wait until Dad gets home," Jess replied.

Dad looked at the box as soon as he came home.

"Good," he said. "It has arrived."

"What has arrived?" cried Zack and Jess. "What is in the box?"

But Dad just smiled again and said, "Wait and see."

He took the big box out to the shed and locked it up inside.

"It will be safe in there," he said.

"What will be safe in there?" said Zack.

"Just let us have a quick look!" begged Jess. But Dad just smiled again and said, "Wait and see."

At the weekend, he spent a lot of time in the shed. Jess and Zack tried to see what he was doing. They offered to help him too, but it was no good.

"Why not?" cried Zack. Dad just smiled, maddeningly, and said, "Wait and see."

At dinner time, he came out of the shed and locked it.

"Did you make something?" said Zack, as Dad came in. "Is it finished yet?"

"And can we see it?" Jess added.

"No, not yet," said Dad. "You can wait and see." He smiled at them.

Zack and Jess tried to peek into the shed, but it was too dark for them to see what was inside.

"What can it be?" said Zack.

"It was a big box," Jess pointed out.

"It was tall but flat," said Zack. "It must be something Dad has to make, as he took it to the shed. But I cannot guess what it is."

So Zack and Jess just had to wait. Dad continued to smile and to tell them to wait and see. At the weekends, he spent a lot of time in the shed, hammering and painting.

Then, one morning, Dad came out of the shed and into the kitchen.

"Guess what!" he said. "I have finished!"

"Finished what?" said Zack.

"I bet we still have to wait and see," said Jess.

"Not this time," said Dad, proudly. "Come and look!"

Zack and Jess did not wait to be told again. They jumped up and rushed outside.

By the shed, Dad stopped and smiled down at Jess.

“This is for you, Jess,” he said to her.

“For me?” said Jess, and Dad nodded. He took them into the shed to see what he had made.

There, inside on the bench, was a little house.

"Thank you, Dad!" exclaimed Jess. "Is it for dolls?"

Dad nodded.

"It is a bit like the one that Jess liked so much when we visited that big old house," said Zack.

"Yes," said Dad. "That is why I made her this one as a present."

Jess and Zack looked at the house. It was painted lavender, with dark stones down the sides. There were tiles on the roof, and inside there were six big rooms.

“All the rooms are painted white,” said Zack.

“Yes,” Dad agreed. “Jess will have to help me decorate them. She can pick out the paints herself.”

"This is like my bedroom, and that is like Zack's," said Jess, pointing to the rooms at the top of the house. "I am going to make them look just like our bedrooms."

"You will need to get a very small bunk bed for your one, then," said Zack, "with lots of little fluffy animals to go on it." Then he grinned. "Do they make small toilets?" he chuckled.

Jess helped Dad to paint all the rooms inside the house. They found some old bits of carpet that they cut down to size. When they had finished painting it, Dad helped Jess take the little house into her bedroom.

Jess spent a long time sitting and looking at her house, thinking about it.

"I will have to start collecting things to go in it," she said to herself. It was going to be fun choosing all the things to go inside. "Perhaps I can make some little quilts to go on the beds," she said aloud to Rags.

Just then, Zack came in. He was carrying a small box.

"Dad said to give you this," he said. Jess took the lid off the box. There inside it was a family of little dolls.

"They are exactly what I need to live in my house!" cried Jess happily.